5.

A Very Small Rebellion

JAN TRUSS

A Very Small Rebellion

A PANDA BOOK

General
PAPERBACKS

Toronto, Canada

Panda edition published in 1990 by
General Paperbacks

Published by arrangement with
J.M. LeBel Enterprises

Typesetting: Jay Tee Graphics Ltd.

Printed in the United States

for Sally

A Very Small Rebellion

A VERY SMALL REBELLION takes place in Canada's prairie provinces. In the summertime, thousands of acres of wheat ripen under the endless blue sky. Oil and gas are pumped up from the depths of the land to make fuel for millions of people. Cattle ranches share the landscape with refineries and grain elevators, and modern architecture breaks the curve of the horizon. Towns and villages spread out from intersecting highways, and farms are usually no more than a short drive from the local grocery store and hockey arena. Even so, most people from the farms and villages make regular trips to the great cities of the Prairies— Winnipeg in Manitoba, Regina and Saskatoon in Saskatchewan, Calgary and Edmonton in Alberta— where more than two million people live and work.

These are the Prairies that Paul Gautier and Simon and Pearl Buffalo, the young rebels of the story, live in and take for granted. It is only when their way of life is threatened that they discover some of the history of the Prairies and the role that was played in that history by Canada's greatest rebel, Louis Riel.

Of course the Prairies that Louis Riel lived in looked

very different than the Prairies of today. Wheat was not sown by the acre and the deposits of fuel had not yet been discovered. Almost everyone used the plentiful acres as grazing land for horses and perhaps a few cows. Food was gathered by hunting and wages were earned by trapping. In 1860, the entire population of the Red River district, where Winnipeg now sprawls, was less than 12,000, and it was by far the biggest community on the Prairies. There were two hotels to serve the trappers who spent most of their days and nights in the wild, two saloons, and only one school. No road or railway connected the community to the East, and the only means of travelling that way was by following the Red River south into present-day Minnesota to pick up the eastern trail.

The land and the lifestyle that Louis Riel knew seems strange and exotic nowadays. But his spirit, as Paul and Simon and Pearl find out, is neither old-fashioned nor modern, but timeless.

These ruled off passages throughout the text are by Jack Chambers.

CHAPTER ONE

It was the last Friday of the summer holidays. Paul Gautier and Simon Buffalo were pretending the holiday would never end. Next Wednesday they would be going to a new school, to the Junior High in Spraggett, and they were nervous about that.

They were hauling water from the stream when a strange yellow truck swung round the bend from behind the trees and pulled off the road. Three men in bright orange hard-hats jumped from the back.

"Wonder what they want," Paul said, straightening up and squinting his dark eyes against the bright sun.

"Look. They're pointing over here." Simon frowned under his black straight hair and lifted the brimming bucket easily so the muscles glistened in his bare brown shoulders.

The driver got out and looked where the others were pointing across the valley, past the two boys knee deep in a pool at the edge of a swift mountain stream. They pointed towards the little Settlement of rough log houses, up the wooded slope to where the chainsaws at the logging camp were buzzing like giant mosquitoes.

"Look! The men are unloading things," Simon said as he and Paul climbed out of the stream, hauling the bucket between them.

Paul Gautier frowned in the hot sun, watching the men at the truck. Drops of water fell from his curly black hair and he had to blink them away. He carried his share of the bucket without strain, and his dark eyes concentrated on the scene at the road.

"Look, they could put guns on top of those things and shoot us up if they wanted," Simon said. He was always reading war comics. He made the rat-a-tat noise of a machine gun and slopped icy water all over their bare legs. Simon liked playing war games.

"Ouch, look what you're doing, will you. Buffalo! Maybe they've come to make a headquarters here in the mountains: headquarters for a battle," Paul said jokingly and splashed water onto Simon's brown chest.

"Stupid!" Simon said. "Who could they have a battle with, eh? There's not enough people here to have a battle."

4

"Stupid yourself," Paul laughed. "They could have a little battle. Bang! Bang! Shoot-outs all around the mountains. Don't you Indians know anything!"

"Grr!" Simon said in a deep voice and made a fierce face. "Go ask Pearl if you want to hear something sensible."

Pearl, Simon's twin sister, stroked the petals of a big sunflower by the back doorstep. Her dark fingers were long and gentle. She bent her head and let her long black hair hide her face. Pearl didn't speak. She was dumb. When she was five years old she had been very sick, and from that time on she had not spoken.

"Don't you Indians know anything, Pearl?" Paul teased. Then he looked serious and said, "There's some men in a truck down by the bend. We're going down to see what they're doing after we've watered the carrots. Coming, Pearl?"

Pearl went everywhere with Simon and Paul, like a dark and beautiful silent shadow. She followed them down the sunny garden path between the tall raspberry bushes as they hauled the bucket to the rows of carrots. While the boys slopped the water along the rows, she pulled up three fat carrots and rubbed the dirt off on her cut-off jeans. With a shy smile she handed one to each of the boys and nibbled on the other herself while they all walked back to the house. Paul tossed the water bucket on the back steps. Then the three wandered slowly in the hot sunshine, munching carrots, along the rutted trail. With the Settlement dogs following close behind, they walked towards the yellow truck.

"Indian kids," one of the men from the truck said as he watched the three walking down the trail.

"Yep. Squatters' kids. See all them houses? No right to be there. Just squatters' houses. They don't own the land the houses are on, see! Those shacks will all have to be bulldozed out, that's for sure."

"Hi," one of the men said as Paul and Simon drew near the truck. He was a young man and when he took off his orange hard-hat to wipe the sweat from his forehead, his hair was yellow and curly. "You live down there?" he asked kindly, nodding his head towards the Settlement of little log houses.

"Yep," Paul answered. He was always the one to speak first.

The young man seemed interested. He leaned on the fender of the truck and asked, "Have you lived here for long?"

"Yep," Paul said again. "We've lived here all our lives. Never lived anywhere else." He wondered why the young man wanted to know.

Simon and Pearl were watching another man carry a tall tripod towards them from the back of the truck.

"What's that?" Simon said quietly, as if he were asking Paul.

"It's a transit," the young man said. "We're surveyors. We've come to plot out the road."

"What road?" the boys asked together, and Pearl crept up behind them to listen.

"The new road that will go from the lumber campsite to Rainbow at the main highway," the young man told them, nodding back towards the campsite half a mile behind the trees, and pointing west across the forest.

"Road through here?" Simon asked gruffly and pointed at the little Settlement houses where washing was hanging on clotheslines in the sun and little children and dogs were playing on the grass.

"Guess that's about it," an older surveyor joined in.

"It'll make a good road to the logging camp," the young man said awkwardly.

"Guess you folks'll have to be clearing out," the older man told them roughly and spit on the grass.

"But we've always lived here," Paul burst out and his eyes flashed. He was thinking of his new bedroom with the shelves and the built-in desk his father had made him because he was going into Junior High school. He was thinking of his mother's big garden with its bright flowers and juicy raspberries.

"Too bad, kids," the man said. "You won't be living here this time next year, that's for sure!"

Two of the surveyors had stretched a tape across the rough track, and the young one was busy looking through the transit. He turned and looked at the children and they could tell he was embarrassed.

"Why does it have to go here?" Paul demanded.

"Yeah. Why can't you move the road over a bit and leave us alone?" The boys sounded rude and angry. Pearl was pressing her hand against her lips and her eyes seemed to be trying to ask a question.

"It's got nothing to do with us," the older man muttered. "We just do what we're told, what the government tells us. You've got the best part of a year to move out. Work won't start on the road till spring."

"You could easily put a bend in the road," Paul shouted. "What difference would it make?" Paul was shaking with anger. "You don't have to go right through our houses."

"New roads have to go straight for safety," the young man with the yellow hair said softly without looking up.

"You Indians got no right to be living here anyhow,"

said a rough man with shaggy eyebrows. "Why aren't you on the Reserve where Indians belong, eh?"

"Because. Because we were here first," Simon shouted, which was strange because Simon never shouted at anybody. Tears had made Pearl's eyes bright.

"Aah, git off home to your shacks. Git out of our way. We've got work to do," the rough man said, and all the dogs started barking.

"You wait till we tell our dads," Paul shouted back.

Pearl flipped her carrot top towards the man and it fell with its ferny leaves spread on his big dirty boots.

But what could they do?

They turned around and walked back down the trail, back to Paul's house and sat on the steps by the sunflowers his mother had grown so carefully.

"We won't let them do it," Paul kept saying. Simon held his head in his hands. Pearl sat very still watching the clouds in the blue sky above the distant mountains.

"We've got to think of a way to stop them," Paul kept saying.

Before May 12, 1870, Canada ended just a few miles west of Lake Superior, at what is now the western boundary of Ontario. Beyond that, stretching from Hudson's Bay to the Rocky Mountains, was the territory called Rupert's Land. The population was very small and most of the land was uncharted. The only people who knew its river valleys and woodlands and grasslands where the Indian nations that had hunted the buffalo across it for centuries.

Rupert's Land was the ancestral home of those Indian nations. They did not believe that land should be divided by national boundaries and then subdivided into private property as the European nations did.

To the Europeans, this land in the New World appeared to be unpossessed. So the English arranged to take "possession" of the territory in terms that conformed to their own ideas about land holding. In 1670, Charles II granted a charter to his cousin, Prince Rupert, to establish a fur trading company on the lands that were drained by rivers flowing into Hudson's Bay. According to the charter, the officers of Prince Rupert's Hudson's Bay Company were to be the "true and absolute lords and proprietors'' of this vast territory.

The Company sent its men, mainly Scottish adventurers, to set up trading posts and work trap lines. Furs were plentiful, and the profits in Europe were enormous. Soon, another fur trading company, the North West Company, began sending their men, mainly French Canadians, into Rupert's Land to trap and set up posts.

The hired hands of both companies quickly learned that survival on the land was no easy matter, and most of those who survived their first winter did so by learning from the only experts at survival in Rupert's Land, the Indians. They camped with them long enough and rode with them often enough to eventually rival them in their knowledge of the land. Many of them married Indian women, and their children represented the spirit and the style of the new land. They could prepare pemmican for the long winter, and they could haggle with the Company factor on nearly equal terms, and they could speak Cree or English or Saulteux or French as the situation demanded. Like the Indians, they were at home in Rupert's Land.

CHAPTER TWO

By the time the men and women returned home from the logging camp that night, the road was marked right through the Settlement with red plastic ribbons on thin sticks. Some of the markers were in the tall grass right against the houses—like bright red flowers.

Paul, Simon and Pearl were waiting for their parents to come home. They waited for their trucks to come chugging down the dusty trail. When they finally did, Paul was up and shouting even before his father and mother could get out of the truck. "Look! Look where they're going to build a road!" He pointed to the red plastic ribbons waving in the evening breeze.

All the men and women jumped down from their trucks and gathered in a muttering crowd by Gautier's house. They were all looking and pointing to where markers stood near their own houses, right up against little windows and doorways.

"Oh no! Surely they wouldn't build a road right through our Settlement. Not through our homes!" Jean-Paul Gautier, Paul's father, said angrily in his French accent. He pushed the thick dark hair from his forehead.

"Sure they would," Simon growled.

Simon's father, who was brown and big as a grizzly, shook his fist at the red markers. "They better not try to build their road through here," he muttered threateningly.

"The surveyors said you can't argue with the government," Paul told them and Simon nodded in agreement. Pearl went and put her arm around her mother who was crying.

"Just look!" Marie Gautier, Paul's mother cried out, "They have already broken down my raspberry bushes putting their wretched sticks right through my garden." There were tears on her cheeks.

All the men and women looked from Marie to Jean-Paul. He was the leader because he had been the first one to build his home in the Settlement. Simon's father spoke up, "Well, Jean-Paul, what are we going to do?" he asked gruffly.

Jean-Paul's eyes flashed. "Mon Dieu," he said. "We

have to do something and pretty quick. But let's be reasonable. I can't believe they will do this thing to us. The government would not turn us out of our homes." He began to speak comfortingly. "No," he murmured, looking at the women who were crying. "If they knew about us, the government would not do this thing. Let us have a meeting at my place as soon as we've all eaten."

It was agreed, and the people went away to their own homes to make supper over hot wood stoves.

"No water, Paul?" his mother asked as soon as they got into the kitchen. "What am I supposed to make supper with? And no potatoes peeled!" Her eyes flashed. "And the stove nearly out!"

"Well," Paul answered sheepishly. "I guess we were watching the surveyors and thinking of things to make them mad. The dogs kept pulling their red plastic stuff off the sticks. Boy, did they ever get mad!"

"Now, I'm mad, Paul Gautier. Get out there and fill the bucket," his mother said sternly.

When Paul came back from the stream, his mother and father were talking quietly in the kitchen. "It's just what I was afraid of," Jean-Paul was saying. "As soon as they got the road as far as the campsite, I guessed they'd want to push it through to join up with the highway at Rainbow."

"That's what the surveyors said they were doing," Paul said. His parents looked at him as if they were annoyed.

"Get that wet dog outside, boy!" His father was after him now.

"And you might have wiped your feet," his mother said tiredly, looking at the muddy tracks on her grey linoleum. "What's the good of me trying to keep the house nice?"

Paul moaned as he mopped up the floor while his father put a cloth on the table and his mother started the hamburgers sizzling over the wood stove.

"Oh surely, they won't mind moving the road over a bit, when they realize this is our home," Marie said hopefully, as her face grew flushed over the hot wood stove.

Paul was setting the table. He paused as he turned to his mother. "But Maman, they said they couldn't change it. One of the men said we should get back on the Reserve where we belong."

Jean-Paul grunted. "Mon Dieu," he said angrily, "I don't see why any of us should be pushed around in a free country anymore. It's like the olden days."

And that's what all the men and women kept muttering when they came to the meeting after supper, crowding into Gautier's big kitchen. Some of the people had lived in the Settlement for as long as twelve years, clearing the trees away, the pines and the bushy poplars. They had built sturdy cabins with thick log walls. Smoke from the wood stoves rose up and joined the mists in the mountains and at night the light from the oil lamps made the windows look cosy. This little Settlement was their only home. Jean-Paul had been the first to build his house, thirteen years ago.

"How can they turn us off our own land?" Simon's father argued.

"They will say it's not our land," Jean-Paul said sadly. "They will say we never paid for it and never got papers to prove it. They will say we are just squatters." The neighbours listened and nodded their heads.

"But I think the government will listen to us," Jean-Paul said, smiling, his dark eyes flashing. We must write to the government and explain that we have made this place our home. We must explain that we have good jobs at the logging camp and that our children will be going to the Spraggett school. We must ask the government to bend the road just a little and leave us in peace. Surely the government will be reasonable and listen to us."

"At least they can't tell you Métis to get back to the Reserve," Simon's father muttered with a helpless grin. Jean-Paul smiled back at him weakly as he sat down at the kitchen table to write the letter to the government. Marie lit the oil lamp and put it near him. The people of the Settlement, some Métis, some Indians, watched while he wrote and explained to the government how important their homes in the Settlement were. When he had finished, the eleven men and eleven women signed their names under the names of Jean-Paul and Marie Gautier.

"The government will have to listen to that," Simon's father said and stood up to go. "When all of us sign the government has got to listen!"

Paul, Simon and Pearl were sitting on Paul's bed watching through the doorway. They hardly dared look at each other because they felt so sad for their parents. The three of them did not believe that the government would listen to the people of the Settlement.

"We must have a plan of our own to move the road, just in case," Paul said softly. Simon and Pearl nodded in agreement. Their dark eyes were very serious.

The children of the white trappers and their Indian wives naturally played a special part in the development of Rupert's Land. Unlike the Indians whose way of life flowed from a tradition of centuries, and unlike the white factors who guarded their Company's interests before all else, the racially-mixed children grew into men and women who saw both sides and understood them.

They were sometimes known as half-breeds, especially if they were of Scots ancestry, but eventually this term became a racial slur and the term that they preferred was Métis, which originally referred only to those of French ancestry. Their common occupation and similar backgrounds led them to band together. They established permanent settlements near the trading posts, where their wives could work together while the men were away trapping and their children could be raised together.

By 1860, they were by far the dominant population in the Red River district. Of the 12,000 inhabitants, nearly half were French-speaking Métis and another 4,000 were English-speaking Métis.

Among them was Louis Riel, Sr. He was a miller, the son of a Québecois trapper who had come west to work for the Hudson's Bay Company. His mother was a Métisse, born in Québec of a French-Canadian father and a Montagnais mother. Riel Sr. was a hard-working and ambitious man who had been sent to Québec for an education. Upon returning to his Red River home at the age of 26, he became a spokesman for his people and a leader in the community.

The year that he returned, he married Julie Lajimodière, the daughter of a famous Voyageur. Julie was a strong woman like her mother, the first white woman to live in Rupert's Land. Married to Riel Sr., Julie presided over a household that was the storm centre during the crises that threatened the Métis people from season to season. She had nine children and she taught them to be proud of their heritage and their native land. She sang to them and read to them and discussed religion with them, and she saw to it that they received the best education that was available to them.

Naturally, the entire community assumed that the first Riel child, also named Louis, would someday inherit the role of leader. They would not be disappointed. Louis Riel was destined to lead them through crises that would change the shape of Canada.

CHAPTER THREE

"Well. Here we go!" Simon said nervously as he caught up with Paul on Wednesday morning. The time had come for them to go to the new school.

"Walk fast if you want to catch the schoolbus," Paul said to the gang of little kids who were following close to Pearl. The little ones were going to the Spraggett elementary school. They were all holding on tightly to their new lunch pails. Pearl had her hands up the sleeves of her new red parka, hugging her lunch pail and her new binder to her chest. It was not really cold enough for her new parka but she had really wanted to wear it the first day to school. She had a new dress too and her long black hair shone like the wings of a blackbird in the morning sun.

"This year we'll have the truck tracks to walk in when

the snow gets deep," Paul said. He was nervous about going to school in Spraggett with the white kids. He didn't know what white kids would be like. "It's going to be easier going to school this way than it was walking across to the Reserve," he said. Every other year the children had gone to school on the Indian Reserve that was close to the Settlement. "We would never get truck tracks to walk in, other years," Paul said.

"And we had more than a mile and a half to walk," Simon added. "Now it's only half a mile to walk to the schoolbus." Simon too was talking to hide his nervousness. But, suddenly, he shouted to everybody, "Hey! Look! Stay in the track."

The yellow truck had swung round the bend from behind the trees and was coming towards them with the men in the orange hard-hats sitting in the back.

"Force it off the path," Simon shouted excitedly.

All the kids stood in the way of the truck.

"Git out of the way," the ugly man roared.

"Move!" the driver bellowed steering with one hand and his head out of the window.

But the kids stood firm.

"Yaa — Yaa," they all shouted when the truck had to make a sudden turn to miss them. It bounced over bumpy roots and the men were nearly jolted out of the back.

Everybody burst out laughing when the men shouted at them angrily.

"Serves you right," Simon yelled.

"Yaa — Yaa!" Paul called after them and all the little kids joined in, walking backwards, watching the truck until it disappeared into the forest.

Paul and Simon had changed since the coming of the yellow truck. Simon used to be quiet and Paul polite. Now they shouted until the truck was out of sight.

"Come on. Better hurry," Paul reminded them and they all ran to the wide gravel road by the campsite where they were to meet the schoolbus.

All the kids who were already on the bus were quiet when the driver called to the Settlement kids, "Come on you guys. Jump in. Find a seat."

It stayed just as quiet while the driver turned the bus around to go back down the road.

Everybody was staring at the kids from the Settlement.

Paul had a seat to himself. A thin girl with straight yellow hair and pale blue eyes sat in the seat across the aisle from him. She stared at him then called loudly, "Hey. You guys off the Reserve?"

"No," Paul answered and felt shy. "We're from the Settlement."

"You Indians?"

"No. I'm not. They are," he nodded at Simon and Pearl and the little kids. Then he pointed at Pearl and blurted out—he didn't know why—he just blurted it out because he was nervous. "She can't talk. She's dumb."

"That's not a nice thing to say!" The girl tossed her hair. "I suppose you'll say all girls are dumb. Dumbbell yourself!"

Paul felt himself go red under his brown skin. Simon and Pearl did not move. They looked straight ahead at nothing.

Paul looked out of the window and pretended not to care, tried not to look at the skinny girl.

But she wouldn't leave him alone. "What's your name?" she said loudly so everyone in the bus could hear.

"Paul," he said and felt silly.

"Paul," she mimicked the French way he said it. "Paul what?"

"Paul Gautier."

Everybody was listening. Paul felt mad.

"Paul Goat," the girl giggled. "They'll call you Goaty."

"Well, what's your name, girl?" Paul's eyes flashed at her.

"Henrietta," she told him.

"Wow! Some name! Henrietta what? Tapeworm?"

"Henrietta Sutmuller," she said and put her tongue out at him. "See! My father came from Holland."

Simon looked round quickly and mumbled, "Suppose Henrietta Buffalo!" It wasn't loud enough for anyone else to hear. Paul and Simon laughed at their private joke. Pearl just sat very still looking straight ahead.

"Well, where are you all from if you're not from the Reserve?" Joe, a boy with red hair and freckles, called from the back of the bus.

"From the logging Settlement," Paul explained patiently. "Half a mile from where the road ends."

"Squatters! My dad says you're going to be bulldozed out of there," an ugly voice said from the seat behind Paul. "None of you never paid for that land. Squatters!"

Paul turned round to look. Simon turned too, and stared into the face of Larry Barnes. He was fat and big with a bulgy pale face.

"If you're not an Indian, then what are you, Goaty?" Henrietta was at Paul again.

"Métis," he said. "See. **MY** great grandfather came from France."

24

"He means he's a halfbreed," Larry Barnes butted in sourly.

"Sure he's a halfbreed," Simon spoke now in his deep voice. "What are you?"

"He's Larry Barnes," Henrietta giggled.

"Him stink." Simon said it like an Indian on television.

Everybody giggled.

"Why are you coming to Spraggett school?" Joe asked from the back of the bus.

"Because it's nearer than the other school, now that they've made a road as far as the campsite," Paul told him.

"We got to get civilized like you guys," Simon said sarcastically.

"What do they call you? Big Chief?" It was Larry Barnes again, sneering.

"He's Simon," Paul said quickly trying to make peace.

"Simon Buffalo," Simon boomed in his deepest Indian voice. "And watch out Lardface or I just might sit on you."

"Squish!" Henrietta said and the other girls giggled.

"This is Pearl," Simon said, ignoring the giggles. "She's my sister. She doesn't talk, see! But she hears. So watch out, see!"

"What grade are you all in?" Henrietta asked, sounding a bit embarrassed.

"Grade seven," Paul told her. "All three of us."

"Me too," Henrietta said. "And Larry Lardface too." She pointed at him and giggled.

"Bet we're going to have some fun this year with you guys," she laughed. "Bet it's going to be different! Come on, we'll show you where to go," she said as the bus pulled up to the doors of the Spraggett school.

The first day had begun.

The hope that Louis Riel would someday be a great leader was not only held by his Métis neighbours. His teachers at the little elementary school at Red River recognized his potential very early and suggested that Louis be transferred to a seminary in Montreal, for more advanced training. Since the Riel family could not possibly afford to send him, Archbishop Taché of St. Boniface arranged for his board and education to be sponsored by a wealthy Montreal family. As much as he hated to leave his home and his family, Louis realized that it was too good an opportunity to pass up. In 1858, he set out with two other boys from his school and one of their teachers on the thousand mile trip that would take him south into Minnesota and then east to Toronto and Montreal. He was only fourteen years old at the time.

By chance, the party met up with Louis' father as they were on their southward journey. Louis Sr. was just returning from a business trip into the United States, and their chance meeting was counted a blessing by both of them. As it happened, that was the last time they would ever meet. Louis' father was to die suddenly six years later while his son was still in Montreal.

The life of a student in a seminary, where boys begin preparing for the priesthood, was particularly difficult, but it seemed to suit the young Riel at first. He graduated from the Junior Seminaire de St. Sulpice and went on to the College de Montréal. He was a solemn and serious student, especially noted for his eloquence in debate. And everyone noticed his piercing dark eyes, which he fixed on the person he was speaking to as if he wanted to look right through him.

When he received the news of his father's death in 1864, he seemed to lose interest in his studies. The next year, in his final term at the College, he decided to quit. He then trained to be a lawyer, but after two years as a clerk in a Montreal firm he quit that too.

Confused and uncertain, he decided to head westward in search of his vocation. He crossed into the United States, stopping occasionally to earn enough money so he could continue his journey. Then in St.

Paul, Minnesota, while working as a sales clerk in a general store, he came into contact with some Métis trappers from the Red River district. They were bubbling with the news from his homeland. The Canadian government wants Rupert's Land, they said, and the Company is going to turn it over to them. There are already signs, they told him, that the Canadians are ready to move in and kick the Métis out.

Suddenly Louis Riel's years of confusion and uncertainty were over. He packed his bags and completed his journey home, arriving in December 1868. He had been away for ten years.

CHAPTER FOUR

"Hi, Goaty," Simon nudged Paul as they hopped across the ruts in the grass on the way home at the end of the first day in school.

"Shut up, Big Chief," Paul said, trying to trip him. But he slipped on the grass and dropped his own books. All the kids laughed.

The dogs from the Settlement came barking and bounding happily to meet them.

"Pretty nice school, eh?" Simon said thoughtfully, while Pearl was twirling round and round dancing with her new books, her red parka flying open.

It had been such a good day that everybody had forgotten the road and the surveyors. Nobody even looked at the red plastic markers blowing in the breeze.

"Miss Pointer is a real bossy teacher, isn't she?" Simon said.

"But I like her—I think," Paul answered and Pearl smiled. "She can talk French as fast as my father."

"She's so bossy, she'll probably make us be in her play for that Drama Festival," Simon moaned.

"Well, she says she always wanted to do that play. She says it needs Métis and Indians to make it good enough to win in the festival," Paul talked on and remembered Miss Pointer's sharp black eyes. "She's a fierce lady, but she must be okay because everybody wanted to do drama for an option."

"You're lucky," Simon said. "You got her for French as well. Why couldn't I get a teacher for Cree? I could easily pass in Cree. Don't know about passing in art!"

"Miss Pointer says the art class gets to make the scenery for the play."

Simon frowned, but Pearl's eyes shone. "I don't know how to make scenery. Bet Pearl will be good at it. She can draw anything. But—not me!"

"Henrietta says you'll be okay. She knows everything, doesn't she?"

"Henrietta skinny pole," Simon chuckled.

"Let's go put up this poster Miss Pointer gave me," Paul said as the little kids ran off to their homes.

"Teacher's pet," Simon sang. "Teacher gave you a poster—because she likes you moster." He pushed Paul so he nearly fell in the middle of the sunflowers. Pearl frowned at them as though to say, 'Boys!', and she pushed open the thick log door into Gautier's cool kitchen.

"Jealous, that's all you are, Buffalo! Jealous because teacher didn't give you a poster," Paul teased and plonked his books and lunch pail with Simon's and Pearl's on the wooden table.

"Let's look at it. The teacher said you've got to look like this guy," Simon said taking off the elastic and unrolling the poster. "Here Pearl, you hold it up."

Pearl took the large poster and held its bright colours up against the pine wall at the bottom of Paul's narrow bed.

"It's wild, Paul. Who did she say that man is?"

"Can't you read or something?" Paul pointed, "look, stupid. Louis Riel, 1844-1885. That's what it says!" He ran his fingers over the twisty orange and brown letters across the bottom of the poster.

"So what! Who's Louis Riel?" Simon shrugged and stood looking with his head on one side into the blazing eyes in the face on the poster. "He looks angry," Simon said.

"He's the Métis guy I'm going to be in the play.

That's how my dad's eyes look when he's mad at something. I got to practise looking like that, Miss Pointer says. That's why she gave me the poster so I can start practising right away.'' He shook his hair until it was rough like the man's in the poster. He picked up the new ruler from his desk top and machine-gunned Simon. "Tat-a-tat-tat-a-tat." Simon fell on the bed and pulled Paul on top of him.

While the boys wrestled, Pearl got some tape from Paul's shelves and taped the poster up neatly on the wall. She ran her fingers along the strands of wild hair and touched the face gently. She liked the man in the poster, with his deep, sad eyes.

The poster shone in the dark. Whenever Paul woke in the night, those eyes were shining down at him and he read the writing until he knew it by heart — LOUIS RIEL, 1844 to 1885. It was creepy in a way, and in a way exciting. It was as though Louis Riel had come to live in Paul's house. The poster was the first thing he saw when he woke in the mornings, and the last thing he saw before he fell asleep at night. Those deep angry eyes looked right down at Paul and seemed to smile.

Paul shook his hair to make it wild and he practised the sad expression, because Miss Pointer said that was the way he had to look in the play. But what could make Louis Riel so sad and angry? Paul wondered.

Sometimes his father, Jean-Paul, came in and stood looking at the poster. He stood up straight and tossed his head.

"What made Louis Riel so sad and angry?" Paul asked him.

"He is sad for the Métis people. He was our leader. He is angry when the government doesn't listen to our voices," Jean-Paul answered. "Mon Dieu, he had a proud spirit."

One night Paul dreamed that there was another meeting in the Gautier's kitchen and that Louis Riel was there talking to the people. He was urging them to plead, to reason with the government, to fight for their homes in the Settlement. His eyes flashed and his words were proud: "You must stand up for your way of life in the forest and protect it against the dangers that menace it." It was a very real dream and when he woke up, Paul felt sure that the man in the poster had come alive.

When Louis Riel returned to his home at the Red River, the rumours he had heard in St. Paul were verified. Canada was indeed negotiating with the Company for the transfer of Rupert's Land. However, their negotiations were by no means settled and when they were, the transfer would still have to be approved by the British Parliament. After that there was the formality of its official proclamation by Queen Victoria. Even the most optimistic Canadian officials predicted that it could not be all settled before December 1, 1869, almost a year away. Until then at least, Rupert's Land would remain an independent territory. There was time enough for the Canadians, if they were willing, to discuss the needs and the rights of the settlers who had been living there for two or three or more generations.

But the Canadian government had other priorities. Most of all they were worried that the United States would move into Rupert's Land and claim it for themselves. As their negotiations with the Company dragged on, the Canadian government grew impatient. They decided to send in their delegates ahead of time. But instead of sending in officials to confer with the settlers, as the settlers had requested, they sent crews of surveyors.

The farms at the Red River settlement had been laid out by the Company according to the scheme used in Québec. Each farm had between 500 and 1,000 feet of river frontage and extended two miles back into the prairie. Beyond that was another two-mile strip of grazing land that belonged to each farm but was generally pooled together to make a large open meadow for common use. The river access was important for shipping goods to the factor and for irrigating cultivated areas; the long ribbon of land was fine for horses and cattle, and it assured that homes would be close enough together to make the families secure during the weeks and months when the men were in the wilds.

The instructions of the Canadian surveyors completely ignored the existing homesteads. It had been decided that Rupert's Land should be resurveyed according to the scheme followed in Ontario. The entire territory would be divided into rectangular sections of 800 square acres, regardless of river frontage.

The settlers protested, not only because the new survey would wipe out their present holdings and, at best, replace them with less desirable lots, but also because any survey at all was premature. They had not given their consent, or even been consulted, and until that happened the Canadians were trespassing on foreign soil. The only result of their protest was that the surveyors shifted their work to the west, beyond the farmland.

However, the surveyors forgot about the open strip of grazing land at the back half of the farms and soon found themselves back on private land. The owner, André Nault, a white farmer from Québec who had married into the Riel family, objected vigorously, but the surveyors simply shrugged and said they could not understand French. Nault ran for help. That afternoon a group of sixteen unarmed Métis approached the survey crew. The broad-shouldered young man leading the Métis stepped down on their chain.

"You go no further," he said quietly, in English.

The surveyors looked up at him, ready to argue. Then they saw the pride in his face and the resolution in his dark eyes. Their arguments caught in their throats and evaporated.

"You go no further," Louis Riel said again.

CHAPTER FIVE

It was nearly winter, when one day a letter came to the Settlement from the Government. It was in answer to the letter that the Settlement people had sent when the surveyors first came.

The letter said that the road must go straight through the Settlement. The Government was sorry, it said, but the people of the Settlement had no legal right to be there. They would have to be out of their houses by the end of April next year.

"It's not right," Simon's father said gruffly. "We were here first."

"The Settlement is our home," everybody muttered at the meeting in Gautier's big room.

Paul and Simon and Pearl listened. They sat on Paul's bed and kept looking into the angry eyes of

Louis Riel in the poster. Paul told Simon and Pearl about his dream and how Louis Riel had talked to the people and told them to stand up for their rights.

"He's right. We've got to stand up and fight for our rights," Simon said looking right at Louis Riel. Pearl and Paul looked at him too.

"Tomorrow we'll change the path of the road," Paul whispered. "We'll move the markers so the road will not go through the Settlement."

"Yes, tomorrow we'll do it," Simon whispered back.

"Just the three of us," Paul said as he and Simon and Pearl put their heads together to make their plan. "We'll have to measure it out carefully. Pearl, you bring a role of string to measure with." Pearl nodded with her dark eyes shining.

"Only the three of us," Paul warned. "Nobody else must know. Nobody must see us doing it."

"Then it will only be us who get into trouble if they find out," Simon whispered.

"Who could ever find out?" Paul whispered back. "When the men come to build the road, they will simply follow our plan. They will put the road where we moved the markers to. They will never know we moved them."

Simon and Paul and Pearl could hardly sleep that night. They were making real plans to save their Settlement.

But during the night, the first snow came, covering everything.

Next morning as the children walked to the school bus they saw the red ribbons of the road markers like bright blood on the new snow.

"We have to make sure we move every last one of the markers," Paul said thoughtfully to Simon and Pearl.

"And we have to get it all done before the ground freezes. I sure hope it doesn't freeze today, while we're in school," said Simon.

"It had better not freeze! We could never move the markers if they got frozen in the ground. We'll have to get the whole thing finished tonight. It all has to be finished tonight before everything is frozen," Paul said as they hurried against the snow.

"We'll get it all done. We'll change the path of the road," Simon said and started running.

"We'll save the Settlement," Paul said and raced against Simon.

They raced to see who would get to the bus first. Pearl won.

When the Métis stopped the surveyors at Nault's farm, they won the respect of most of the Red River community. The English-speaking Métis, after all, felt as threatened as their French-speaking neighbours did: their own holdings could disappear when the aloof new governors took office. Even the resident officials of the Hudson's Bay Company, still the governors of the territory, seemed relieved to see the surveyors leave. They too felt that they had been overlooked in the negotiations between the Company and Canada. Not only were they not to receive any part of the £300,000 that Canada would pay for the new land, but all they could look forward to was a sizeable decrease in the lands that provided their furs when the Ontario farmers began to arrive. Moreover, William Mactavish, the chief factor of the Company and the Governor of Rupert's Land, had obviously given up any effort to govern. His power had been totally undermined by the negotiations going on without him in Ottawa and London, and now he was gravely ill—in fact, as everyone knew, he was dying.

Riel realized that to assure themselves of their rights, his people would have to earn Canada's respect. Clearly they did not have it now, and clearly it would not be earned as long as the people did not have an active political body to speak for them. In a series of meetings, he filled the political void in Rupert's Land by setting up the National Committee of the Métis of Red River.

It was set up along the lines of the traditional Métis organization for the annual buffalo hunt. Officers were elected by a consensus that judged them on their natural talents and past achievements. Ambroise Lépine, the best marksman and rider, became General. He assembled 500 armed men for the militia, charged with patrolling the trails to keep out any further intruders. John Bruce, an experienced leader in the hunt, was named President, though everyone knew that his talents in the hunt would not serve him as well in this venture. It did not really matter, however. Riel, too young to be President, was elected Secretary, but everyone expected him to do the work of both offices.

It would take a bold act, Riel knew, for the men in Ottawa to take the Committee seriously. As it happened, Canada's newly-appointed Lieutenant Governor of Rupert's Land, William McDougall, was enroute to the Red River district at that very moment. McDougall's reputation preceded him, and his appointment was ominous for the Métis. He was already hated in Québec as an opportunist from Ontario who appealed to the anti-French, anti-Catholic feelings that existed in some areas of that province. Still, Riel saw McDougall's premature arrival as a political opportunity. He drafted a letter to be presented to McDougall at the border. It was in French, and it said simply: "The National Committee of the Métis of Red River orders Mr. William McDougall not to enter the Territory of the Northwest without special permission of this Committee."

Since McDougall had no authority whatever in the territory until the transaction between the Company and Canada was proclaimed, the Committee's action could not be considered revolutionary. On the other hand, the Canadians seemed to have assumed sovereignty all along, so the action would almost certainly shock them. And in order to receive the "special permission" to enter the territory, all McDougall had to do was begin serious discussions with the people about their future citizenship within Canada.

The letter could result in cooperation, or in a collision. The choice was McDougall's.

CHAPTER SIX

That day, school seemed to go very slowly. Simon could not keep his mind on his work. "I hope it doesn't freeze!" he whispered to Paul and looked out of the window at the grey sky during the math lesson.

"Any more talking from you, Simon Buffalo, and you can stay in after school and walk home," Mr. Plotsky shouted. Simon wasn't very good at math. Mr. Plotsky was always losing patience and shouting at him. Once already he had kept Simon in after school so he missed the school bus and had to walk home. It was a long way. Paul didn't want Simon to be in trouble and have to walk home tonight of all nights. He passed a note saying. "Keep out of trouble. You've got to be home early tonight. Remember!"

But the day seemed so long. Paul couldn't keep his

mind on school any more than Simon could. He kept drawing plans of where they should move the markers so the road would miss the Settlement yet still look straight when the roadbuilders came.

As they were changing classes to go to drama he caught up with Simon and said, "It isn't freezing. The snow's gone all squashy. We're going to be all right."

"I saw you making plans," Simon told him. "Where do you think is the best place to make the road go?"

"I think the best plan is to make it go north of the houses. But we'll have to move a lot of markers, about half a mile back into the bush, I reckon, to make the road look as though it joins on straight."

"Wow! Half a mile back into the bush. It'll take us all night," Simon said and wished the long school day would end. He went grumbling into drama class.

It had never seemed much like drama. Miss Pointer was very strict. She said that in a play you had to be able to pretend. First she made them do all sorts of drama exercises, crazy things like walking proud and walking sad, quarrelling without any words, screaming without any sound, carrying heavy things that weren't there. Then when they had practised all those things and a thousand more, she still said, "No, we can't start the play until you've got the history straight in your heads." She explained that a play was make-believe, and the play they were going to do was a pretend way of showing the proud spirit of Louis Riel. The proud spirit—that's what his father had said, Paul remembered. Miss Pointer said they should get some of the history straight so they would understand the play better.

She still hadn't given out the play books. It was more like a social studies class than drama. Everybody was fed up and grumbling.

Miss Pointer made them make maps of the way Canada had been more than a hundred years ago. Canada! It wasn't Canada from sea to sea. Then it was only Ontario, Quebec, New Brunswick and Nova Scotia. The play was going to be about that time before the West was part of Canada.

"But—a hundred years ago!" Simon kept muttering to himself.

"Who cares?" everybody grumbled and sulked.

Just because Pearl was nice and quiet and never caused any trouble, she got to make a great big map to cover a whole wall. She was good at things like that. She did things just the way she felt like doing them. Pearl had a mind of her own.

She made her map of the West before it was part

of Canada. She painted the Red River blood red because Miss Pointer once said that the Ojibwas and the Sioux Indians, a long time ago, had battled on its banks. And in the Red River she made two big riverboats. Pearl was really good at things like that. Everybody kept looking at her picture map. But Sam Schultz, who was always showing off, mocked Pearl when she put the name Winnipeg in neat red letters on a tiny village in the middle of the gold prairie on her colourful map. "Winnipeg!" he mocked.

"What are you laughing at, Sam Schultz?" Miss Pointer asked sharply while Simon glared. Simon didn't let anyone laugh at Pearl.

"Anybody knows Winnipeg's a railroad centre. All the tracks meet and cross there," Sam Schultz sneered.

"Yea! And it's got skyscrapers," Larry Barnes called out.

"A hundred years ago?" Miss Pointer asked. "Pearl knows what she's doing!" she said. "Pearl, you make a list on the board, and show these boys the only things Winnipeg had a hundred and ten years ago."

Pearl went shyly to write on the blackboard. Everyone watched as she wrote in her careful writing:

In 1869 Winnipeg was comprised of:
    riverboats

1 butcher shop
1 flour mill
1 gun shop
1 harness store
2 churches
2 beer parlors
1 hotel
1 newspaper shop
1 photographer's shop

"Yikes," said Chrissie, who sat in the front row. "Is that all there was then? We went there last summer. Now it's a great big city you could get lost in."

Miss Pointer laughed. "Pearl really finds things out," she said. "See on her map how Fort Garry was a more important place than little Winnipeg. The Hudson Bay Traders used Fort Garry for a head-quarters and kept all their supplies and ammunition there. See the wall round the fort, and the places for the guns that Pearl has drawn in?"

"Bang, bang," Sam Schultz shouted because he always had to show off. Only a few students thought he was funny.

Simon was sprawled on his desk looking bored. He didn't care anything about a hundred and ten years ago, or a hundred years ago, or even ten years ago. He was thinking about his own home, the Settlement.

Miss Pointer sensed that the class was restless. "It's time we started the play," she said, and began passing out the thin paperback books that had the face of Louis Riel, the face from the poster, on the cover.

William McDougall, the first Lieutenant Governor of
Rupert's Land, was stout and round-shouldered and
short of breath. Most of his life had been spent in political arenas and backrooms, places where a man is not
likely to improve his physical condition. As a young
man, he had trained to be a lawyer, but he worked
mainly as a political journalist, until he was elected to
the House of Commons from Ontario. In politics, he
had risen quickly: he was in the group that negotiated
the union of Nova Scotia, New Brunswick, Québec and
Ontario to form Canada in 1867, and he was Minister
of Public Works in Sir John A. Macdonald's first
Canadian cabinet until his appointment as Lieutenant
Governor.

McDougall never hid his political prejudices. He was
a white Protestant of English ancestry, and he firmly
believed that Canada would be a better place if everyone else was like him. The people who elected him—
also white Protestants of English ancestry—shared his
belief and supported him strongly.

His duties as a cabinet minister consisted almost

solely of promoting the expansion of Canada into Rupert's Land. He urged it in resolution after resolution in the House and in a series of insistent letters to the British government. Not only was it necessary to annex the territory, he argued, but it was essential to make Canada's intention clear to the Americans right away. He had sent in the survey crews prematurely for that purpose. Now he himself was on his way to begin his administration, also prematurely. His travelling companions included his four teen-aged children and some friends from Ontario who would be his key aides in Rupert's Land. They were there, they all assumed, to witness the high point of McDougall's political career.

When they were met at the American border by the Métis couriers with the letter forbidding him to go any further, McDougall was livid. Was he not, he sputtered, the Queen's representative? Who did these half-breeds think they were anyway? Why should he care about their ridiculous letter—so curt and simple-minded, and in French? He pushed the couriers aside and rode on to a Hudson's Bay Company post two miles inside the border. A little later an armed patrol of Métis led by Ambroise Lépine pulled up at the post and calmly began putting the Canadians' belongings back into their carriages. When that was done, they ordered the Canadians to climb aboard, and escorted them back to Pembina, on the American side of the border.

For almost a month, McDougall flooded Ottawa with letters requesting further instructions, but the Canadian government's replies were very cautious. After all, McDougall still had no jurisdiction in the territory and they could hardly intervene because of the treatment he had been given. The whole situation was so explosive, they felt, that the proclamation would have to be postponed until the government could look into it more closely. But postponement was the one event that McDougall would not stand for. In his mind, the date for the transfer of the land to Canada was December 1, 1869, and it would not be later, even if he had to write the proclamation himself. In the end, he did just that, claiming Rupert's Land for Canada and appointing himself—"our trusty and well beloved William McDougall"—as Lieutenant Governor. At the bottom of the page, he carefully copied the signature of Queen Victoria.

On the night of December 1, he and six of his party harnessed the carriages and made their way to the post inside the border. It was twenty degrees below zero that night, with a bitter wind blowing the snow in dense clouds. McDougall and five of the others formed a circle. One held the Union Jack, which was whipped by the wind and lashed at their faces. McDougall had trouble grasping the proclamation because of his heavy mitts, and the light from the flickering lamp was so bad that he kept losing his place. His lips were so cold that the words could not be understood, and his voice was barely audible over the howl of the wind.

The seventh man in the party, a resident of Rupert's Land, huddled in one of the carriages and watched with disbelief. He could hardly wait to get back to Pembina and describe the scene to his friends. The next day, the spectacle of McDougall freezing in the wilderness as he read his own proclamation was on the front page of the local newspaper. From there it spread to every newspaper in North America. William McDougall became known everywhere as the leading clown in a hilarious political farce. It was the end of his political career.

CHAPTER SEVEN

"Now you must remember," Miss Pointer reminded them, "that a play is a pretend way to catch the spirit of the way it was. And, Simon Buffalo," she said loudly because he had his head down on his desk, "you read the beginning, page five. You can be the Indian."

Everyone giggled. An Indian for an Indian. That was funny. Then everyone became silent as Simon's deep voice read the words seriously, words from a hundred years ago:

"This land. This is my land. Look at my land, my country, fertile of soil and fair to look upon."

Larry Barnes snorted. "His land!" he said rudely. Miss Pointer looked furious. Somebody nudged Larry and others said, "SHHHHH. Shut up."

"Go on, Simon," Miss Pointer said.

He went on reading, his deep Indian voice getting deeper. Everybody listened. "My land stretches in peace to the quiet horizon. My land. My land is a prairie of flowers blowing in the wind, tiger lilies wild, the shy rose shedding its scent, the wild pea and the morning glory, the black-eyed daisies dancing."

Pearl was standing very straight against the bright prairie on her map. Her eyes were shining. She looked very proud. The room was hushed.

"But that was a hundred years ago," Miss Pointer said quietly. "How can we make a stage seem like Simon's prairie of a hundred years ago, to catch the spirit of the time?"

"We can make clumps of flowers on thin wire stems," Henrietta said. "And Pearl can paint a background scene like her map with Winnipeg and Fort Garry," Chrissie added.

"And we have to be thinking about the sound effects too," Miss Pointer reminded them and told Simon to go on reading his part.

Simon read proudly, "My land. Land of the free wild life. Duck flying. Kildeer calling. Geese. Prairie hens scattering in flocks. Oh listen, listen to my land. Listen to the galloping thunder of the buffalo herds."

Somebody in the class made the sound of geese honking across the sky. Somebody else made the little twittering sounds of prairie hens scattering.

"Good," Miss Pointer encouraged them.

At last the play was beginning.

Somebody started to drum on the desk top with his finger tips. It sounded like hooves beating. Other people caught on to the idea of making the massive sound of a buffalo herd thundering across the prairie.

"Okay! Okay!" Miss Pointer had to shout over the galloping hooves. "Let it fade away. That's a really good idea. If we use microphones it will take only four or five of you to make good sound effects.

She explained to them that, in the next scene, workers for the Government of Canada come onto the stage. They come on with transits. Does anyone know what a transit is?"

"You bet we know," Paul and Simon both said.

"What are they for?" Miss Pointer asked.

"For plotting the path of a road," Paul told her.

"That's right, and also for measuring the land. Measuring the free wild land to divide it into private farms," Miss Pointer said.

Then the class read how, just over a hundred years ago, surveyors from the Government of Canada went to the free wild place where the Indians and Métis had their homes by the Red River. The surveyors were sent to divide the land into farm and house lots. But the new lots were not for the people who had lived there for so many years. These Métis and Indian people learned that their land was to be sold. The Hudson's Bay Trading Company was selling their land to the Canadian Government. The Government would then offer the lots to new settlers, most of them from Ontario.

The surveyors were measuring these lots and putting their markers right through the long narrow strips of land that went down to the river. Each family farmed a narrow strip of land which was bordered by the Red River. But the surveyors cared nothing for the way the people there lived. They marked the land into sections and squares so that many squares had no river frontage at all. The surveyors behaved as though the Métis and Indian people had no right at all to their free wild life on the Red River.

"This is creepy," Simon whispered to Paul. "It's like a play about our own Settlement."

"Only a hundred years ago," Paul whispered back. "Sure, it's creepy!"

And the Métis and Indian people were angry and afraid, the play said. They cried out, "We will not let this thing happen. We want to keep our free wild life, where the buffalo roam and men are hunters. We will stand up for the right to our own way of life." And the people called for a man named Louis Riel to be their leader.

Louis Riel had been away to university in Québec. He would be able to reason with the government. He would be able to fight for the rights of the Red River people.

"Louis Riel, lead us. Louis Riel, speak for us," the Métis and the Indian men and women in the play called.

"That's the guy in your poster, 1844 to 1885," Simon whispered to Paul.

Miss Pointer heard him. "Yes, that's right," she said. "AND Paul is going to read the part of Louis Riel."

Paul remembered his father had spoken of "the proud spirit of Louis Riel." He put the proud and angry look in his eyes and read, "You mean the Hudson's Bay Trading Company is selling this land, our homeland, our homes, without asking us. They are measuring our land, our free, wild land—"

Sam Schultz was reading the part of one of the government roadworkers who was named Scott. "Nobody has to ask halfbreeds for anything! Squatters!" He read the words and sneered.

Joe, with the freckles, was reading the part of a chief surveyor who wasn't such a bad guy. He read, "Mr.

Scott, please don't speak like that to the natives."

Sam Schultz was supposed to spit.

Simon, as the Indian, read again, "It is our land. We were here first."

"Rubbish!" It was Larry Barnes reading the part of a Canadian trader. "Bah!" he read, "You only have the use of this land because the Queen of England lets you."

"No," Simon grunted.

"Yes," shouted Sam Schultz, as the roadworker Scott. "All of this land belongs to our Queen, believe me. Even you belong to the Queen of England. So do the buffalo that graze upon these plains, and the fish that swim in the rivers and the song of the birds in the trees—they all belong to the Queen of England, and if she says the Canadian Government can buy this land—it can—see!"

"No," Simon grunted again. "How can that be? Who can own the song of a bird in the tree? No!"

Paul then read fiercely, "He is right. One person cannot own another. The good Queen has never interfered with our way of life. I am convinced that she will listen to us. We have a right to speak and say what shall be done with our land, what shall become of our way of life. I shall lead my Red River people to speak for themselves, to stand up for their rights. We will speak to the Government of Canada and to our Queen."

"Halfbreed!" Sam Schultz, as Scott, shouted. "Who do you think you are to talk of being a leader? Halfbreed!"

Larry Barnes read cunningly, trying to persuade the Métis and Indians to give up their land peacefully. He talked slowly as though the Indians and Métis could not understand English very well. "White man come as brother," he read, saying each word carefully. White man come not as conqueror, he come like brother.

Simon grunted. "White man's tongue crooked as the horns of mountain goat!"

Everybody laughed. Simon sounded so funny.

Then they all laughed some more at the scene in the play.

Even Simon had forgotten for a moment that he wanted to get home and move the road markers.

In a crazy part of the play, a man called McDougall was supposed to come to the Red River land and be the Lieutenant Governor for the Canadian Government. But he was afraid. He believed the natives were dangerous. He stood on the border between the Red River land and the U.S.A. and tried to claim the land. In the play he was a weak and silly man, a figure of fun. The cold made him shiver so much that he could only stutter the words, "I-I-I hereby-by de-de-declare th-th-th- this land-dd-d-d to be-be-belong to Can-Can-Canada in the n-n-n-name of. . ."

The funny man never finished claiming the land for the Canadian Government because a few Métis and Indians frightened him away. McDougall was so afraid of the Métis and Indian people that they did not need guns to drive him off. They clapped their hands and shooed McDougall and his men away as though they were silly chickens. The scene was meant to be a funny part in the play. Miss Pointer said that every good play needs funny parts to balance the serious parts.

When the bell rang, everyone grew quiet, waiting for Miss Pointer to dismiss the class for the day. Paul tossed his head. He felt like Louis Riel. He felt like a rebel against the Government. Paul thought it would be great to be a leader of his people like Louis Riel. The feeling stayed with him all the way home on the bus.

"Charge! Charge!" he yelled as they got off the bus after the long day at school and ran towards their Settlement through the soft white snow.

"Charge! Charge" Simon yelled. They ran home with all the little kids following yelling, "Charge! Charge!" Pearl waved her arms and ran among them.

After the little kids had run on to their own homes, Paul huddled with Simon and Pearl. "Let's change our clothes quickly. Let's be quick and get started on standing up for our rights," Paul said urgently to Pearl and Simon. "The government will not change our free wild life!"

"Charge! Charge!" Simon yelled.

"Into battle!" Paul called. "Move the mighty road! Charge!"

During the six weeks that William McDougall spent pacing and fuming at Pembina, the Red River settlement became more and more tense. The English-speaking population, both Métis and white, wondered which side they should take in the dispute. So far, they had remained neutral in spite of the many editorials in the local newspaper advising them to join with the Canadians against their French-speaking neighbours. The viewpoint of the newspaper was clearly not that of the majority, and in fact the so-called 'Canadian faction' which controlled it was a small group of men known to be old friends and acquaintances of McDougall who could be certain of prospering if he ever took over. But the Canadian faction at Portage la Prairie, the other major settlement in the area, was larger and tougher.

One reason for the tension at Red River was the supply of 300 rifles that McDougall had brought with him from the east. The English-speaking settlers had not attempted to arm themselves so far because Riel moved tirelessly among them, explaining the actions of his

National Committee and justifying them. Only his eloquence was keeping the community together, and his friends wondered how long he would be able to keep up the pace. Moreover, there were more rifles close at hand. Fort Garry, which housed the headquarters of the Hudson's Bay Company, held 390 rifles in its arsenal, and its entrances were only loosely supervised now by Governor Mactavish, who lay there dying.

On September 2, 1869, the same day that McDougall and his travelling companions were escorted back to Pembina by Ambroise Lépine, Riel and 120 of his men quietly took command of Fort Garry. Mactavish himself had unofficially suggested that they do so, knowing that he could not offer any resistance and fearing that there would be civil war if the Canadian faction got there first.

Riel now controlled the military stronghold at Red River, but he wanted most of all to unite the rest of the community in the cause. He invited the English-speaking parishes to elect twelve representatives and form a council with twelve elected representatives from the French-speaking parishes. Meetings began immediately at Fort Garry to review the situation, and on December 1—the day that McDougall read his proclamation in the icy blizzard a few miles away—the council agreed on a proclamation of its own. Among other demands, they would require the Canadian government (a) to respect the privileges and customs of its new territory, (b) to recognize both French and English as official languages in its legislature, (c) to provide grants for schools, roads and public buildings, and (d) to grant the new territory fair representation in the Canadian House of Commons.

This proclamation was called the "Bill of Rights", and the people of the Red River district were justifiably proud of it. Its demands were nothing out of the ordinary; they were merely statements of what might reasonably be expected by people who had a lifestyle and traditions of their own. McDougall, they knew, would never agree to it. They could only hope that the Canadians would soon send more reasonable men to deal with them.

CHAPTER EIGHT

They had to work fast. It would soon be dark. They felt like rebel adventurers as they hurried through the bush, north of the Settlement, and began to take out the markers and plot the change in the road. They were beginning where they thought no one would see them. It had to be their secret. They had decided that they alone must take responsibility for moving the road. "Stand up for the rights of our people like Louis Riel said," Paul proclaimed as they dug out the first marker.

They looked like three Eskimos in the snow-filled forest as they pulled their fur-lined parka hoods almost over their faces. The wind was frigid. With numb fingers, Pearl stretched the measuring string between the trees, measuring as carefully as she could because their road had to be exactly as wide as the road the surveyors had planned.

"They'll never know!" Simon said through cold lips, as he dug at a marker with a spade. Underneath the snow the ground was hard. "A different crew builds the road, not the same men who did the surveying."

"They'll just follow our markers," Paul laughed as he banged one down in the place Pearl showed him. The red ribbons blazed in the rising wind.

As they worked the wind grew more and more fierce. It drove through the pine trees, tugging at the string as Pearl stretched it from tree to tree. Inside her gloves, her fingers were stiff and aching with cold. The wind got louder and filled with snow.

"It's blowing a blizzard," Simon shouted through the hiss of the wind and the creaking of trees.

"Good! Nobody will see us," Paul shouted back and kept on working with determination. It was icy cold.

"Look, our tracks are already covered," Simon yelled and pointed like a snowman to where the earth around the last marker they had moved was already covered with white.

They had to cling to each other as they fought to move against the lashing wind and blowing snow.

Although they were icy cold they kept on working. In the blowing snow it was hard to see—but they kept on working, moving the markers, pounding them in their new places. By the time they were dodging around the Settlement it was almost dark. Nobody saw what they were doing.

At last they were down by the campsite moving the last marker over just a little way, so their road looked straight. They pounded it in. The last one! They clung together and fought their way back to the Settlement.

The snow covered their tracks.

"There'll be no school tomorrow if this snow keeps up," Simon said.

"But this blizzard is starting at exactly the right time for our plan," Paul shouted as they pushed against the gusts of wind with their heads down. "Nobody will notice what we've done. Nobody will notice!" They hugged each other in the cold biting wind. They had done it! They had moved the markers to make the road miss the Settlement. They had done it! They were standing up for the rights of their people!

Paul and Simon and Pearl were frozen but very, very happy.

Paul was right. Nobody did notice that the markers were gone from the Settlement. It wasn't just that the snow had covered everything, it was also that everybody was too busy to think about the road and the markers and things that were going to happen next year. Everybody was busy trying to keep warm, trying to keep the day-to-day life going. The deep snow made life in the Settlement very difficult. It was hard to keep warm round the little wood stoves. It was hard to bring in firewood through the deep snow. It was hard to get the trucks to start. It was hard to get the washing dry.

The blizzard was just the beginning of a long cold winter. So much snow! Spring seemed far, far away. The problem of the new road coming through the Settlement seemed far far away. So nobody noticed the markers were gone.

But throughout the long winter Paul and Simon and Pearl smiled secret smiles thinking how happy everyone would be when the road builders followed the new path of the markers and the new road missed the Settlement.

Louis Riel earned the respect of his people during the year that he spent with them. When he had left he was just a skinny fourteen year old who liked to read books. He returned three-quarters priest, one-quarter lawyer, and nothing definite. Now he was twenty-five, a sturdy man, but he had never chased the buffalo, he could not shoot a rifle accurately, and he would surely die if he had to tend a winter trap line. Still, when the political troubles grew serious, he knew exactly what to do. He knew better than any priest or lawyer, and better than any leader they could remember—better even than his father. They made him the President of the National Committee.

He had known somehow it would be all right to move his men into the fort where the Canadian faction could not surprise them. Governor Mactavish had never even protested. His aides on the Committee supplied him with the background he had missed during his ten years away from Red River, and he gave the Committee direction and confidence. The community council squabbled sometimes, but at least it gave all the people a chance to voice their opinions and speak their minds. And it had settled on the Bill of Rights, that list of courtroom words that made a person feel proud to be from Rupert's Land.

Now the community council took on an official title, and an important one. They declared themselves the Provisional Government of the territory. With Mactavish incapable of governing and the Canadians unauthorized to govern, someone had to maintain order and protect the people's rights. Only the community council was representative of all the people. Louis Riel was not only the president of the Métis but, for the time being at least, the president of all the people. Surely the Canadians would have to confer with him before they took their next step.

CHAPTER NINE

The first warm day came late in March.

Paul and Simon and Pearl felt excited, not only because it felt like Spring but because tomorrow, Saturday, was the day of the Drama Festival at the Central School. They were in Paul's room on Friday afternoon when Jean-Paul and Marie Gautier got home from work. The sun was still shining. The long icicles all round the eaves of the log house were dripping and melting.

"It's Spring! Spring is coming!" Paul greeted his parents gaily.

"Spring. Mon Dieu!" Jean-Paul said bitterly. "I never thought the day would come when I would be sad to feel Spring in the air. To think what Spring means to us, this year!" He sighed.

"There's still a lot of snow and ice to go yet," Marie said sadly, looking out of the window across the deep snow that still covered her garden. "There is time for more snow. There is even time for the government to change its mind and move the road."

"The time for change is running out. We can't pretend that Spring will never come. It will come, soon now. The government will not help us, I feel it in my bones," Jean-Paul said angrily and despairingly.

"Oh cheer up, Papa," Paul laughed. "I think they will take the road past the end of the Settlement. Don't you, Simon? Don't you, Pearl?"

"Sure," Simon said and Paul smiled.

"Why look!" Marie burst out. She was looking out of the window. "Why look! Perhaps the children are right. The markers have gone from my garden!"

Paul and Simon and Pearl ducked into Paul's bedroom and laughed into the eyes of Louis Riel. They nudged each other and listened to what Marie and Jean-Paul were saying.

"More likely the markers are broken off under the snow," Jean-Paul said uncertainly.

"No. No. I think they've been moved. Oh, Jean-Paul, I feel certain the government would never be so cruel as to make us leave our homes. No. I know! They have changed the plans."

Louis Riel looked down at Simon and Paul and Pearl. He seemed to smile. But Marie's words had brought tears onto Pearl's cheeks.

Paul called to his parents, "It's the day of the play tomorrow, remember! Miss Pointer says it's a good play. She says we have a chance of winning."

"I'm scared I'll forget my words," Simon kept saying. "Pearl doesn't have to worry about that," he said.

He meant that Pearl had no words to forget, of course. But she had a part. She was the Great Indian Presence. She had to stand on a tall stool in the background, dressed in long robes and a magnificent headdress of eagle feathers. She had to be the 'Silent One' watching over everything.

"Well, it had better be a good play. We've heard so much about it!" Jean-Paul teased.

"It's got to be the best play," Paul said and shook his hair and made his eyes look deep and brooding like Louis Riel's.

"We have to win because our play is true," Simon said and Pearl nodded in agreement.

Jean-Paul lifted his head and his eyes flashed. "You have to win for Louis Riel," he said. "To keep alive the proud spirit of Louis Riel."

Suddenly the Canadian faction, the small group of men in Rupert's Land who urged annexation by Canada under any conditions, sensed defeat. Some of them had hoped that they would be given good positions when the annexation came. They had started the newspaper of the territory and expounded their views relentlessly in its pages. They included doctors, lawyers and merchants, men of means who felt their hopes and plans slipping away from them. The Canadian government, they heard, was more interested in Riel's activities than in theirs. If things kept on this way, it would soon be sending delegates to meet Riel and discuss his bill of rights.

Perhaps all was not lost, however. The number of men who wanted Canada to come into the territory had grown somewhat in the past few years, as young men from Ontario had come with road building and surveying crews and then stayed behind to stake a claim for farmland on the prairies. Most of them arrived with a prejudice against the Métis, and they burned inside when they had their government jobs cut off by them.

They would prove to be dangerous enemies for Riel when they were organized, and the time was ripe for getting them organized.

Dr. John Schultz, the outspoken leader of the Canadian faction, armed 48 of his angriest followers and moved them into his big house a few miles from Fort Garry. They made a great display of barricading the windows and doors, hoping that they might win over some of the neutral white settlers by showing their determination. The settlers were as unimpressed as the Métis, who referred to the house as "Fort Schultz," but Riel and the other leaders knew that they would have to take decisive action to prevent bloodshed. Riel surrounded the house with a force of 300 men and ordered Schultz to surrender. When he refused, the Métis rolled up two cannons and aimed them at the front door. That was enough to persuade Schultz's men to throw down their arms.

As the prisoners were marched into the jail at Fort Garry, Riel must have thought that the territory's internal problems were now solved. He could not have guessed that one of those prisoners, a young man who swore and spat at his Métis captors as he went along to jail, would limit Riel's political career and destroy his peace of mind for all the rest of his days.

CHAPTER TEN

Two bus loads of parents from Spraggett went to the Central School for the Drama Festival.

A lot of people from the Settlement were there too.

The large auditorium was packed with people standing at the back and at the sides.

Paul, Simon, Pearl and all the Spraggett Junior High kids began to tremble with stage fright after they had watched four good plays done by other schools. While the fifth play was in progress they had to go to the dressing rooms to get ready.

They wanted to be the very best. But they were all shaking as they lined up at the sides of the stage behind the curtain.

A man's voice, like a hollow ghost, made the announcement: "The students of Spraggett Junior

High will now present a new Canadian play." The voice paused and then boomed, "A VERY SMALL REBELLION."

The curtains were opening.

It was beginning.

Sounds of wild geese and ducks and the coming of the thunder of the hooves of the buffalo herd—the play had started.

The buffalo herd faded away into the distance.

Simon, the Indian, walked in among the swaying clumps of flowers in front of the painted grey walls of Fort Garry and the little village of Winnipeg.

Simon raised his hand and said in his low, low voice: "This land. This land is my land," and immediately a deep silence fell on the audience.

The audience didn't seem to breathe during the scene when the men with the transits measured the prairie stage and Sam Shultz, playing the part of the man called Scott, was terribly rude. He had to spit and yell "Halfbreed" and "Squatter" at Louis Riel. It was very rude, very ugly, very real.

Somehow, Paul had become the Louis Riel on the poster. His black hair seemed to fly from his head and his black eyes flashed in anger.

"Halfbreed! You call me halfbreed. Yes. I am Métis and I speak the proud French tongue of my adventurous forefathers who loved this wild and beautiful land. My land. Land of the Métis people and homeland of the Indian. Homeland of our mothers.'' Paul's voice rang clearly through the crowded auditorium so that everyone in the audience sat up straight to listen.

Louis Riel cried out, "The Government must listen to us who live on the wild face of this noble land. The Government must ask *US* what *WE* want."

The crowd on the stage was dressed mostly as Métis men and women in flowing fringed leather. Some were Indians and some were farmers in their work clothes.

Now they all crowded around Louis Riel and sat among the swaying summer flowers of the prairie near the stone wall of the fort. And the crowd called like a thousand voices, "Riel. Riel. Lead us. Riel lead us."

A Métis woman called out, "Lead us against the invaders who drive away the buffalo, who put fences on our wild land."

Louis Riel called out and lifted his arms, "They SHALL ask us what we want."

"We must keep our own French language."

"Yes. Yes," the crowd roared.

"We must keep our own religion."

"Yes. Yes," the crowd roared again.

"The Métis people must have land to call their own."

"Yes. Yes." The crowd agreed and stood up and cheered.

Louis Riel's voice grew stronger and rang around the auditorium. "We must be asked how we shall be governed," he cried.

"We are capable of governing ourselves," "Why should we allow them to send out whichever politician THEY think fit to govern us? Why? Why? Why?"

The crowd swayed with the flowers and cheered. "Why? Why? Why?" they chanted. The prairie flowers danced on their stems.

Riel walked away and the crowd followed chanting in a long procession, "Riel, Riel our leader. Our leader."

Right then the audience clapped very loud although it was not the end of the play.

The new year, 1870, promised peace and prosperity. Canada's delegation arrived at Fort Garry to begin negotiations. Later that winter, the talks were shifted to Ottawa, and by late spring agreement had been reached. The new province, named Manitoba by Riel, was granted most of the demands in its Bill of Rights, including 1,400,000 acres of farmland for its Métis inhabitants. For Riel, it should have been a time of fulfilment, but he could not pause to enjoy it. He was facing the greatest problems of his presidency.

Among the prisoners in Fort Garry, by far the most obnoxious was Thomas Scott, a young man from northern Ireland who had served in the Canadian army for a while in Ontario before coming west as a road builder in a Canadian crew. He lost that job when he tried to drown his foreman because of some wages he claimed he was owed. He joined Dr. Schultz's enforcers in Fort Garry and waited eagerly for some action.

As a fanatical Orangeman, Scott had been taught to loathe all Roman Catholics, especially French ones, from the time he was born. He found it especially easy to hate the French-speaking, Catholic Métis, who were challenging the supremacy of Scott's allies. In his jail cell, he screamed abuse at the guards all day long, daring them to shoot him and calling them cowards when they did not. Several of the guards must have been secretly relieved when he escaped from the jail and temporarily disappeared.

Unfortunately, he was not gone long. He joined the Canadian faction in Portage la Prairie as they were gathering a force to storm Fort Garry and release the prisoners. As they marched from Portage la Prairie towards Fort Garry, stopping at every farm and settlement to recruit more men, Scott made himself conspicuous by boasting to everyone who would listen that he would kill Riel with his bare hands. Only when the force got closer to Fort Garry did they begin to learn about the real strength of the Métis army. Their mission, they were told at farm after farm, was suicidal. Soon the ranks depleted, slowly at first but in droves later, when they were within sight of the fort. The attack had to be called off.

Scott and some of the others were bitterly disappointed. In a futile gesture of defiance, they paraded fully armed within sight of Fort Garry. The Métis troops quickly surrounded them and put them under arrest. Scott was in prison again.

This time he was worse than ever. He shouted and

screamed and banged on the bars of his cell. He assaulted the guards at every opportunity. Worst of all, he incited the rest of the prisoners to do the same, threatening to kill them along with Riel if they followed the prison rules. Finally, the guards could stand it no longer. They demanded that Riel court-martial Scott before he started a riot in the jail. At his trial, Scott did nothing to help his defense. He shouted and swore, and pledged to kill Riel when he was freed. He sneered at the Métis officers who were his judges and said that they were afraid to sentence him to death. But they did. By a vote of four to three, they found him guilty and sentenced him to face the firing squad.

At noon on March 4, Scott's eyes were covered and he stood before his executioners. Three of the six Métis marksmen held rifles loaded with real bullets, and three shot blanks. None of them knew which rifle he held, but when the signal to fire was given, three bullets found their mark.

In Ottawa, the Manitoba Act was almost ready to be read before Parliament. In its name and in its spirit it was the creation of Louis Riel. But in Ontario his fame spread for a different reason. He was the "murderer" of a white Protestant from Ontario. Thomas Scott would be avenged.

CHAPTER ELEVEN

The rest of the play was all in snow, made to look very deep by hanging long strips of soft white cheese-cloth over the prairie flowers. The stage lights were made to shine cold, icy and blue on the white folds of cloth and on the grey walls of the fort.

How the audience laughed at the part where the man called McDougall shivered onto the stage, saying through chattering teeth, "So-so this is the P-P-Prairie Settlement I'm supposed to be L-Lieutenant G-Governor of. My-my g-goodness, its a c-c-cold place," he said to the two men who were with him. "B-but come on! Be-be-be- quick! Let's c-claim this-this land for Canada. Where-where's the Bible," he shook and shivered.

The lights got icy blue to make the audience feel cold.

McDougall was shaking all over now, so he could hardly keep his hand still on the Bible. He began to stutter and shake in the most terrible way. "In-in-in the n-n-n-name of her Ma-ma-majesty the Qu-queen I de-de-de."

It was while McDougall was standing and stuttering that Riel and his men walked in and drove the frightened white men off by merely clapping their hands.

"Go home. Go home, you silly man," Riel ordered.

The man who had come to be the Lieutenant Governor ran away while Riel and his men stood laughing.

"We will not allow Canada to send the people of the Red River a government without our permission," Riel said, suddenly fierce and serious. "My friends," he said, "I pray we never need to fight, but I fear the time has come when we need an army. We must be prepared to defend ourselves. We must be prepared in case Canada sends stronger men than McDougall to lay claim to our land. I do not believe in bloodshed, but we must be prepared. Go, my friends, go and bring out your guns and your brothers. We shall have an army to defend our rights."

Riel's men went off in all directions. Some walked down the aisle through the audience, getting the audience to feel the spirit of men going out to get their guns and their brothers to form Riel's army.

When the crowd of men came back with their guns, the voice of Larry Barnes was heard from behind the wall of Fort Garry. Then his frightened face was seen looking over it. He was shaking and his teeth were chattering. "They're coming. They are going to attack us." Riel and his men came to the gate of the Fort. "We surrender," the men in the Fort cried, and put their hands up in fear although none of Riel's men had so much as raised a gun.

Louis Riel laughed. What was happening was such a surprise.

"Come on, men," Riel called. "They want to give us the Fort with all the supplies and ammunition. Sure, sure, we come in peace," he called to the trembling men of the Fort. Riel started singing "Allouette" and all his men joined in as they walked into Fort Garry. They could still be heard singing when they had all disappeared behind the wall into the Fort.

In the next scene, Riel had his men raise a new flag on the flagpole to fly under the Union Jack. The new flag was white with a French lily on it. The men cheered when it went up. It was to show the spirit of Riel and his people.

But, no sooner had the cheer died than a new force of men was seen coming onto the snowy stage. They were carrying a cannon. And the man named Scott, the rude one, was leading them.

"Halfbreeds! We'll blast them out. We'll show them they cannot take over Her Royal Majesty's Fort," Scott whispered menacingly. His men were creeping up behind the cannon. They were stepping high through the snow.

But the audience was giggling. It was another funny scene.

While Scott and his men crept towards the Fort, Riel and his men were creeping in the other direction along the back of the stage.

Suddenly Riel said, "Drop your guns. Surrender!"

The cannon dropped BANG on the stage snow.

The audience laughed.

Once again, Riel and his men were making the men from Canada look foolish. They drove Scott and the others into the Fort at gunpoint.

"Halfbreed! You'll pay for this! Dirty halfbreed," Scott kept yelling as he was marched behind the wall.

Then the audience cheered because Riel and his men had captured the loudmouth Scott. It was clear that the audience was on the side of Riel and his people, not on the side of Canada.

The audience listened while Scott was tried behind

the wall. His loud voice was heard calling his captors a pack of cowards. He even shouted that he would kill Riel. "You would not dare to harm me," he was heard screaming.

But a horrible silence fell when Scott was brought out by guards with their guns ready. They were going to execute Scott. He was blindfolded. It was horrible.

"Go home, the rest of you. You are free to go," Riel called out to the other prisoners. But Scott was led to the edge of the snow and was made to kneel down.

"This is murder," he screamed.

"We have shown the Government of Canada that we mean business." Louis Riel said sadly. He crossed himself and looked to the sky as though he were praying.

"You'll pay for this. Halfbreeds!" Scott cried again.

"We must make the Canadians respect us," Riel called to the sky, like a prayer.

The firing squad raised its guns.

Simon the Indian spoke. "Louis, dear friend," the deep voice pleaded. "You should not have this man killed. You are foolish. The white man will have vengeance." Simon the Indian spoke sadly.

"Scott is an ignorant man. We shall make an example of him," Riel said firmly. Then he turned and went inside the Fort.

The firing squad shot Scott and he fell heavily to the stage.

The stage went black. The audience was horribly silent.

Simon's voice fell quiet and deep into the silence. "Louis, my friend, you should not have allowed your men to do that," he said. "The white man will revenge the death of his brother."

There was a long dark pause to show that time was passing. The audience breathed quietly, waiting.

Then, a messenger rushed on the stage.

"Riel. Riel, you must hide. Run away. You will be hanged for the murder of Scott. They are after you."

"Louis, my friend. Run. Escape," the Indian called.

Riel, with a pack on his back and a gun on his shoulder crept away in the night shadows, away from the place where he had led his people, away from the Red River.

The Indian was right. The white men wanted vengeance for the death of Scott.

Riel was a hunted man.

The Province of Manitoba came into existence on May 12, 1870. A few months later a warrant was issued for the arrest of the father of the new province, Louis Riel. To escape arrest, Riel was forced to move around from day to day, hiding in the homes of his friends. It was more annoying than threatening for him at first, and it was made easier by his belief that the Canadian government would grant him full amnesty sometime soon.

The amnesty never came. Most of Ontario, and parts of the Maritime provinces too, demanded vengeance on Riel for the death of Scott, and even the hint of an amnesty seemed likely to lose Macdonald many votes. As always, Macdonald was willing to break a commitment to keep the votes.

The Orange faction in Canada was grimly determined to get Riel. The Premier of Ontario announced a reward of $5,000 for the arrest of Thomas Scott's "murderers". Dr. John Schultz, Riel's old enemy, returned to the Red River to swear out a personal warrant for the arrest of Riel for "the murder of Thomas Scott." Now the threat to Riel's life was more serious and he was pursued everywhere by bounty hunters, even south of the Manitoba border.

His people were sick at heart but could do little to

help him. Even with his life constantly disrupted, they elected him three times to the Canadian Parliament as the member for the Provencher riding. By the third election, he was an exile from his homeland; he won without ever setting a foot in his riding during the campaign. They understood, of course, that by electing him they would not have a real representative in Ottawa because Riel would be arrested or killed if he showed up there, but they elected him anyway.

For ten years he was in exile. For a day or a month or a year, he lived in St. Paul, Minnesota, or Montreal or Keeseville, New York, or someplace in between. Frequently penniless, he worked at menial jobs until he thought it necessary to move on. He was depressed for long periods and exhausted from his constant travelling. Finally, he headed westward again as he had done during his earlier period of confusion. He moved to Montana and worked with the local Métis and Indian people there. His life became more settled, and soon after he married and began to raise a family.

While Riel was wandering in a strange land, many of his people found themselves strangers at home. Settlers were moving in daily, mostly from Ontario. The new neighbours were suspicious of the Métis people and hostile toward them. Worst of all, the trapping and hunting grounds were being turned over to the new settlers for farmland, and the great buffalo herds were suddenly extinct. Family after family packed its belongings and headed west for the valley of the Saskatchewan River, to begin again.

By 1884, the Métis settlements were well-established on the new frontier. To the immigrants from the Red River, it seemed chillingly familiar when teams of men began arriving from Canada to make surveys and build roads. Once again it appeared that the Métis would be shoved aside while the Canadian plans developed behind closed doors.

Louis Riel had become a legend among his people. Every Métis man, woman and child could recite his achievements at Red River. Now, in Saskatchewan, trouble was brewing again. They would send for Louis Riel.

They found him at St. Peter's mission school in Montana, teaching the Métis children. As he listened to their story, his dark eyes seemed to grow darker. When they were finished, he nodded. The next morning he packed his belongings in a buckboard wagon and began the long, hard journey to Saskatchewan with his young wife and two infant children. His people needed him, so he was going home.

CHAPTER TWELVE

The audience sat in darkness.

On the stage there was just the light of a thin crescent moon.

Simon spoke into the hushed darkness. His words told how the great Riel, leader of his people, was in exile for ten years.

"But he had been a great leader. The Government of Canada had listened and allowed the people of the Red River to become the new Province of Manitoba."

Riel, leader of his people, was the Father of Manitoba.

"But alas," Simon said sadly, "even the great Riel could not save the free wild life for his people. Roads, and trains, and settlers drove the buffalo and the fur-bearing animals out of Manitoba. The Métis and

Indians who wanted to live the free wild life of hunters and trappers moved westward, westward to where Saskatchewan is now.

But the roads, the railways and the settlers moved westward also.

Again the Métis and the Indian people lived in fear. Surveyors were on their land again with transits, measuring the land. Again the people of the free wild life were only squatters on the lands that had been their home.

In their fear the people called out again to Louis Riel. They knew of no one else who could be their leader.

Métis men and women came onto the stage in their fringed leather garments, quiet in their soft mocassins.

As the sun rose on the stage they began to call, "Louis Riel, you must come, your people need you."

"You are still the hero of your people. They speak of you and pass your name to their children."

"Your people need you badly."

"The buffalo are gone."

"We go hungry."

"The white man spreads west like a river in flood."

"We followed the wild animals for we are hunters."

"We followed the wild land and we ran before the fences."

"Louis Riel, the people need you. The time has come

to fight the white man who destroys our land and our way of life and does not hear our voices."

Louis Riel said quite simply, "If my people need me so much then I will join them. I shall return to help my people again."

There were sounds of rejoicing when Louis Riel returned to his people and there were sounds of fear from the Government of Canada. Canada called out its armies. Canada was afraid that the free wild people might all join together and make a war. Canada was afraid of Louis Riel.

At the Battle of Batoche, Riel was taken prisoner.

The last scene in the play was terrible.

Louis Riel was in the government's jail and he had been sentenced to hang.

He was standing blindfolded with the hangman's noose around his neck.

The hangman's hand was raised.

A hollow voice boomed out, "Louis Riel, traitor to your country, you shall die."

Riel raised his head and spoke softly. "My people are my country. I have never been a traitor to my people. I die at peace with God and man, and I thank all those who helped me in my misfortunes . . . I ask forgiveness of all men. I forgive all my enemies."

The Métis people all around the edges of the stage

were kneeling and murmuring like a little wind, "Louis Riel. Louis Riel."

Pearl, the Great Indian Presence, had her arms outspread in her long robes.

The hangman's hand was moving. Then a shrill cry, like the cry of an eagle, cut across the stage and echoed like a wall around the crowded auditorium. "No! No! No!" the strange voice cried. It was like the cry of an eagle crossing the lonely sky.

"No! Riel shall not die. He shall not die," the voice cried.

But Riel fell dead in the hangman's noose.

And everyone saw that it was the Great Indian Presence with her arms uplifted who had made the cry like an eagle across the sky.

Pearl had spoken.

As though magic had taken hold of them all, the kids on the stage crowded around Pearl and they shouted with her, "He shall not die! He shall not die!"

That wasn't in the play at all.

They were still shouting while the audience clapped and cheered as the curtain came down to end the play.

Before the judges made the announcement, Spraggett school knew that their play A VERY SMALL REBELLION had won.

Riel returned to his people in triumph. After ten years of wandering in exile, fourteen years after leading the resistance at Red River, he never dreamed that such a reception would await him at Batoche, Saskatchewan, the new centre of the Métis colony. Hundreds of people, many of them his childhood friends, converged on his wagon, cheering him and shaking his hand. He greeted them and spoke firmly of the need for unified action to secure their rights: winning title on the lands they occupied, and getting representation in Parliament for the territories of Saskatchewan, Assiniboia and Alberta. Three days later, he repeated his stand in a speech at a white settlement a few miles away and was gratified that the cheers were no less loud there. Soon after that, he spoke at Prince Albert, in the heart of the white settlement, and found more support. With such unity, he thought, the people's rights could not be denied.

The Métis at Batoche were well organized and strongly led. Charles Nolin, Riel's cousin, had been one of his chief advisors at Red River. During Riel's exile,

Nolin became a minister in the Manitoba cabinet and a prosperous businessman. He moved west as justice of the peace and manager of a timbering business. His contacts with Canadian officials would serve the Métis well in the coming confrontation.

The leader of the Batoche Métis before Riel arrived was Gabriel Dumont, a skillful leader of the hunt and the best marksman and rider his people had ever seen. The respect for Dumont's ability in the field carried over to the settlement, where he maintained strict authority. When the confrontation appeared inevitable, it was Dumont who proposed that they send for Riel, a man with experience in such matters, and Dumont was with the party that travelled to Montana to bring Riel north. His decision to send for Riel was political as well as practical. Dumont realized that Nolin had also had experience in dealing with governments but he would not hear of turning over the leadership to him. Nolin, he felt, would threaten rebellion, if need be, in an attempt to open negotiations with the government, but he would quickly back down if the government countered with force instead of talk. Dumont, on the other hand, was prepared to meet force with force if he had to, and he believed that Riel would agree with him.

From the beginning, the government rejected any petitions to negotiate. The land belonged to Canada, they said, unlike the land at Red River when they had been forced to enter negotiations. This time they would govern the land as they wished. After all of the petitions were rejected, Riel formed an army with Dumont as general. The government's response was to double the number of Mounted Police in the territory.

All the while, Prime Minister Macdonald was pre-occupied by other problems. Construction of the Canadian Pacific Railway had slowed down. Macdonald's political dream was to connect the northern continent from sea to sea by this great railroad and bring British Columbia into Canada. Now, Parliament was stubbornly refusing to lend the CPR the additional $20,000,000 it required. There had been scandals about the misuse of funds already lent, involving millions of dollars, and the people were fed up with Macdonald's demands for more.

His dream would never be realized unless he could convince Parliament that a crisis was brewing in the area where the railroad was still unfinished. Later, he would admit that he concocted the crisis to serve his own ambitions. "We have certainly made [the Métis resistance] assume large proportions in the public eye," he wrote to a friend. "This has been done for our own purposes. . . It never endangered the safety of the state." Macdonald spread rumours of war and called up the Canadian army. The railroad, he urged, was essential to transport the army to Saskatchewan.

When the first shot was fired in the west, by a scout in the Canadian militia, the loan to the CPR was quickly approved. Macdonald would have his railroad after all.

CHAPTER THIRTEEN

Everything was so exciting they forgot to think about the road. All they could think about was the play and Pearl finding her voice.

So much was happening.

"Goody gumbo! Goody gumbo!" Henrietta chanted joyfully when Miss Pointer told them they would get next Monday afternoon off school to take their play to Highcourt Central School auditorium, fifty miles away.

"Goody, goody gumbo. We'd never have won if you guys hadn't come to our school," Henrietta said as she danced around Pearl, who watched her seriously.

"Guess you'd just have done a different play," Simon said matter-of-factly.

"No. Not as good," Henrietta insisted. "And I'm

glad we're leaving the end the way we did it when we won, with Pearl crying out like that and us all shouting, 'He shall not die'. That was terrific!''

Paul laughed. "Gosh," he said. "I was so surprised I nearly forgot to die."

"Riel will never die," Pearl surprised them again with her serious rusty voice. She still didn't use it very often and when she did she was very serious.

"That's right," Miss Pointer said. "Heroes never die. They live in each one of us."

Paul and Simon and Pearl straightened their shoulders and smiled. They smiled because they were rebels against the government too. They had changed the path of a road.

"There is another announcement," Miss Pointer said. "Next Friday we will take the play to Edmonton."

Everybody cheered. That meant a whole day off school.

"Next week will be terrific," Henrietta said, jumping up and down. "Monday afternoon off and all day Friday. And we get to meet all the kids from the other schools." Henrietta loved talking to new people.

"Yes, next week will be good," Paul said as he thought of the audiences clapping and cheering.

But other things happened that week too.

On Monday morning, as they walked to the bus, Paul and Simon and Pearl saw the yellow trucks arriving. They were pulling long house-trailers for men to live in. Work on the road was going to begin.

"Soon we shall know if our plan worked," Simon said quietly.

"Yes, let's keep our fingers crossed," Paul said. "With a bit of luck they'll just follow our markers and everybody will live happily ever after."

"Amen," Simon said and crossed his fingers.

That afternoon they performed the play in the Highcourt School and while the audience was still cheering, Paul and Simon and Pearl thought of the road builders and crossed their fingers again. On the way home they had to walk past the long, white trailers where they could hear men's voices and radios blaring. Big road building machinery was parked by the trailers ready to start work in the morning.

"Nobody's noticed," Simon whispered.

"How can they know where the markers used to be?" Paul whispered confidently. "These men didn't put the first ones in. Their job is just to make the road go where the markers tell them to go." Paul sounded very confident. He even stopped whispering. Everything was going to be all right, he felt sure.

But the next day, Paul and Simon and Pearl found they were wrong. They were watching out of the window in Math class when they saw the Mounties drive up to the school.

Then the three of them were called over the intercom and told to go to the principal's office. They looked at each other. They crossed their fingers. They felt their stomachs go creepy.

The two Mounties were very tall. They kept walking about while they asked questions. Mr. Jeffers, the principal, just sat silent behind his desk.

"You really should answer the policemen," he said at last when Paul and Simon and Pearl stood stubbornly looking at the floor, saying nothing.

"Well, somebody has interfered with the roadwork," the Mountie with the moustache insisted quietly.

"I bet the government did it," Paul spoke up at last, bravely. "Our parents all wrote to the government."

"No. We know better than that," the other Mountie said firmly. "In fact, we went up to the logging camp this morning to tell the people they will have to be moved out of their houses by the end of this week."

Simon and Paul and Pearl felt their stomachs cave in and turn over. They wanted to be sick. Pearl's eyes got bright with angry tears. "Our homes!" she cried.

"Those are our homes," Simon said defiantly.

"They have no right to make us move out," Paul shouted.

"They can move the road to follow our markers," Simon yelled.

"So you admit you moved the markers," the Mountie with the moustache shouted back.

Paul and Simon and Pearl just looked at his shiny shoes and said nothing. Nothing. They were so angry they wanted to cry.

"It's a lot of money wasted. Taxpayer's money," the other Mountie grumbled. "Two days' work for four men. That's a lot of money."

"Our houses cost a lot of money," Paul shouted.

"More than just money," Simon shouted too.

"You can't make us move," Paul said.

"Remember your manners, children," the school principal interrupted.

"Your moving is none of our business," one Mountie said. "It's just our job to see the law is kept."

"Your parents will have to know about this," the one with the moustache threatened. "This time we'll let you off with a warning," he said, "because it is the first trouble you've been in. But don't ever do such a thing again or you'll be in serious trouble."

"You just remember that," the other Mountie said looking down at them.

"We'll remember," Pearl's rusty voice rasped.

Mr. Jeffers stood up, nodded and looked down at her.

The Mounties said they could leave and to remember they'd been warned!

Everybody crowded around Paul and Simon and Pearl when they went back to the classroom and Larry Barnes said, "*SEE*, I told you so. My dad said you guys were going to get bulldozed out. You're squatters, that's all."

Paul and Simon and Pearl didn't say anything back. They felt sick. Nobody said anything back. They knew how their friends felt.

All the rest of the day, Paul and Simon and Pearl were desperately trying to think of some way to save their Settlement.

The first shot in the "war" against the Métis was fired by Gentleman Joe McKay. He shot an Indian scout, Assywin, and Isidore Dumont, the brother of the Métis general, from a distance of not more than six feet, killing them both. Isidore Dumont was holding a white truce flag when he was shot.

It happened at Duck Lake, a few miles from Batoche. The advancing Canadian army, made up of volunteers and Mounties, had unexpectedly met up with a Métis battalion led by Gabriel Dumont on the trail. Both sides scurried for cover and lay watching one another. Then Dumont sent his brother and the scout forward with a white flag to find out the army's intentions. The commanding officer and his scout emerged to meet them and after exchanging a few words the officer commanded the scout to shoot. At the sound of the shots, both sides advanced. After half an hour the Canadian army retreated, even though it greatly outnumbered Dumont's thirty men. Twelve soldiers and four Métis died at Duck Lake.

The might of the Canadian army was quickly mustered. At Macdonald's order, 6,000 additional men were pressed into service. They began the trek to Saskatchewan, aided by a railway that pushed deeper into the prairies every day by crews that worked around the clock. The first wave included soldiers, almost 600 horses, eight cannons and two Gatling guns, the first machine guns to be used anywhere in the world.

As the Canadian army inched toward them, the Métis dug a ring of pits around Batoche to protect their riflemen. When the front line of the advancing army was a day away, Dumont took 130 men to meet them and struck with a dozen ambushes and skirmishes. More than half of his men were killed. Dumont and his men headed wearily back to Batoche, and the Canadian army stopped its advance, waiting for more men and supplies.

Two weeks later, reinforced and rested, the Canadian army moved their cannons and Gatling guns to Batoche. The battle began on May 8, 1885, with heavy losses to the army. For the next four days, wave after wave of Canadian soldiers stormed the Métis pits, accepting certain injury and often death to obey their officers' commands. Eventually this plan worked. The Métis ran out of ammunition. Riel arranged a cease-fire in order to give his troops time to escape into the wilderness. The battle was over.

Gabriel Dumont escaped to the United States, where

he earned his living occasionally as a trick rider in carnivals. He returned to Batoche years later and died there in 1906. Charles Nolin had fled before the battle of Batoche and later had the charges against him dismissed because he was the government's key witness against Riel. Riel's wife and children were taken to the home of Riel's mother in Manitoba to wait through his trial and even through three postponements of his execution date. They were never to see Riel again. Immediately after the battle at Batoche, Riel headed towards the United States, but he soon decided to stop and give himself up to the Canadian officers. He had spent too many years running already. Jailed in Regina, he stood trial for treason, was convicted and sentenced to hang. On the eve of his execution, he wrote: "For fifteen years they have pursued me in their hate, and never yet have they made me waver; today still less, when they lead me to the scaffold." The next morning, November 16, 1885, he climbed the scaffold in the police barracks at Regina. At his side, he noticed the priest trembling. "Have courage, father," Riel whispered. Moments later the noose was slipped over his head.

CHAPTER FOURTEEN

The RCMP told the parents about the markers being moved.

"Good. I'm proud of the children," Jean-Paul told the Mounties. "I'm glad they tried a little rebellion. It is a very terrible thing to be losing your home."

The Mounties seemed embarrassed and went away after telling all the people at the Settlement that they must be out of their houses by Sunday night. "You've had plenty of warning," the Mounties said.

"But where do we go, I wonder," Jean-Paul said to Marie. "The government says we can't stay on this land. Where can we go!"

"I can't believe this is happening," Marie whispered.

"It's just the same as in our play," Paul said.

"That's why Miss Pointer made us do the play,"

Pearl explained wisely in her deep strange voice. "That's why we have to do the play better than ever," she said talking slowly.

And on Saturday night, in Edmonton, the Spraggett school did A VERY SMALL REBELLION better than ever. The audience clapped and cheered loud and long.

But the play ended. And the children had to go home. Paul and Simon and Pearl left the school bus for the last time and walked towards the Settlement, to where their parents were waiting with the trucks all loaded with furniture and clothing from their houses. Paul saw his desk and his books in the back of their truck against the old black wood stove.

The road building men were standing beside the big machinery, just watching, chewing their gum.

"It makes me mad," Simon said. His father was pouring gasoline over the doorstep of his house. He threw a lighted match onto it. A sudden roar and blaze!

The other men set fire to their homes. The spring blue sky filled with black smoke.

"Where are we going to live?" Paul whispered to his father. He felt like crying. This was the end. Their little rebellion had not worked.

"We don't know yet where we can live," his father answered sadly but he stood up straight and squared his shoulders.

"Will we still be going to Spraggett school?"

"We don't know yet. We know nothing for certain." Jean-Paul spoke and his eyes were dark.

"Why wouldn't the government listen to us?" cried Paul.

The strange rusty voice of Pearl spoke against the cracking of the burning wood and the roar of the flames. "One day they will listen," she said. "They will all listen." There were tears on her cheeks.

They all lifted up their heads and looked at the burning homes with eyes that were angry and sad like the eyes in the poster. Like Louis Riel.

"Hey, Papa, did you save my poster?" Paul asked suddenly.

"I would not forget Louis Riel," his father answered, and they heard the proud spirit in his voice. He put his large hand on Paul's shoulder and they walked to the waiting truck.

* * *

EPILOGUE

The battle at Batoche took the lives of thirteen Métis—twelve riflemen, and one child. The child was the only victim of the famed Gatling gun. As military losses go, that was a light toll. Yet the battle was as devastating as a massacre in the effect it had on the Métis people.

For seventy-five years the once-proud Métis nation was silenced. Its leaders were gone—Riel executed, Dumont exiled, and Nolin ostracized. Younger men who might have come forward in other circumstances saw too clearly what had happened to the great leaders of their father's generation and hung back. Poverty became a familiar lifestyle for the survivors. It began in the aftermath of the battle at Batoche, when the Canadian officers made no attempt to prevent their men and the white settlers from burning homes to the ground and driving off herds of livestock. The Métis had always lived with minimum supplies and their stores had been depleted by the war effort. The looting and burning meant ruin for all of them.

Even more devastating, in the long run, was the propaganda campaign launched against the Métis people by government officials, newspaper editors, members of the Orange Lodge and other elements of the ruling group in Victorian Canada. Compared to you and me, they said, the Métis are "wild" and "savage" and "uncivilized." Just look at them, they insisted, living in squalor, with no property of their own. Those who understood how the Métis had lost their property and became impoverished could not find any audience for their views. Eventually, the view that the Métis were inferior to other human beings was accepted by a majority of Canadians simply because they heard it so often and listened to it so uncritically.

The result was a wall of racial prejudice that no Métis, no matter how gifted and ambitious he was, could break through. Listen to Howard Adams, a Métis who is now professor of education at the University of California, describe his feelings when he was growing up in Saskatchewan in the 1950's: "Whenever I spoke to whites, I was extremely self-conscious about my halfbreed looks, manners and speech. I was very sensitive about my inferiority because I knew that whites were looking at me through their racial stereotypes and I too began to see myself as a stupid, dirty breed, drunken and irresponsible . . . I hated talking to whites because . . . their attitudes and the tone of their conversation left no doubt about white supremacy" (*Prison of Grass*, New Press: 1975).

Only recently has the wall of prejudice begun to crack. The private documents of many of the Canadians who opposed Riel, especially Macdonald's, are now public, and more and more people are forced to face the fact that what they had been led to believe about Riel and the Métis people was a lie. In the 1960's, a statue of Louis Riel was unveiled at the Saskatchewan provincial legislature in Regina and his story was the subject of a successful play and opera. Recent histories of the period have begun to reflect the view that Riel and his people were the victims of crude and conniving politicians, who were willing to destroy the Métis in order to guarantee that the Canadian Pacific Railway would be completed and that western Canada would be English-speaking. Bit by bit, old prejudices are breaking down.

As the wall cracks, a generation of Métis is forcing

its way through it and into the political consciousness of Canada once again. The Métis leaders assemble annually at Batoche to discuss their responsibilities and rights. Their voice is heard again, with growing unity and strength, as they argue with new governments in a new era about an old issue: their title to the lands they have traditionally held, this time in the Northwest Territories. They may yet find justice in this land. Until they do, people like Paul Gautier and his family will continue to be pushed around because of some arbitrary edict from a remote official.